PO LIN LEE

OPHELIA HOUSE

THE S.I.C. JOB

Palanquin

EXCUSE ME, Giggle.
I AM PO, JUST PO.

CREATED AND WRITTEN

CARLTON L. SAMPSON

ORIGANAL ARTWORK

ANDREW L. WILLIS

PO LIN LIFE

OPHELIA HOUSE
THE S.I.C. JOB

ORIGINAL ARTWORK

ANDREW L. WILLIS

CREATED AND WRITTEN

CARLTON L. SAMPSON
COVER DESIGN, BALLOONS, PAGE LAYOUT

Palanquin

SINGAPORE
CIVIC DISTRICT

COVER: PO IS STANDING ON THE BACK OF A SPACE
SOLAR POWER (SSP) SATELLITE SOLAR REFLECTOR.
THE SSP SATELLITE BACKGROUND ILLUSTRATION
DEPICTS TWO SPACE SOLAR REFLECTORS FOCUSED
ON A CONVERTER-TRANSMITTER. THE CONVERTER-
TRANSMITTER CONVERTS THE SOLAR ENERGY
AND TRANSMITS A MICROWAVE TO A RECEIVING
STATION, RECTENNA ARRAY, ON THE EARTH'S
SURFACE. THE MICROWAVE IS CONVERTED INTO
ELECTRICITY AT THE RECEIVING STATION.

Cracka...ah...ah...ah...ackle,
rumble, rumble,
rumble,
thumb, thumb,
bomb...bomb...
...bomb.

Shpok!

Crisssk!

SOME PEOPLE SAY PROOF OF MAN'S PREDATORY DOMINANCE AS A SPECIES IS NOT CONTINUOUSLY EVOLVING WEAPON SYSTEMS BUT MAN'S PREHISTORIC MASTERY OF THE PLANTS, MINERALS, AND ANIMALS OF HIS ENVIRONMENT; HUMANITY'S INNATE AWARENESS OF NATURE, THE ELEMENTS, THE SPIRIT, OF HOW THEY COMBINE TO MAKE LIFE. AWARENESS LOST TO THE CONTINUING WAR, FAMINE AND PLAGUE OF ANCIENT HISTORY. AWARENESS SYMBOLIZED, RITUALIZED, AND RETAINED AS FAITH BY A SURVIVING PREHISTORIC ANIMISTIC BELIEF SYSTEM. ITS DISCIPLES PERFORMED THE BIRTHING RITE OF THE 'TA SHEN LING', THE 'SHE DEMON', PO LYN LEE. SHE IS THE 'MI CHU', THE 'SECRET DEATH'.

LIGHTNING FLASHED, FOR AN INSTANT DIMMING THE BRIGHT LIGHTS OF SINGAPORE'S DOWNTOWN NIGHTLIFE.

Splish!

Splash!

Splash!

NOBODY REMEMBER ME...

THERE ARE MORE THAN 5000 ACTIVE EMPLOYEES WORKING IN OVER 300 BROTHELS IN SINGAPORE'S OFFICIALLY DESIGNATED RED-LIGHT AREAS WHERE PROSTITUTION IS LEGAL. HOWEVER, IN SINGAPORE CHILD PROSTITUTION IS AGAINST THE LAW. YET AT SOME ADDRESSES THE SITUATION DICTATES, AND THE LAWS DO NOT APPLY.

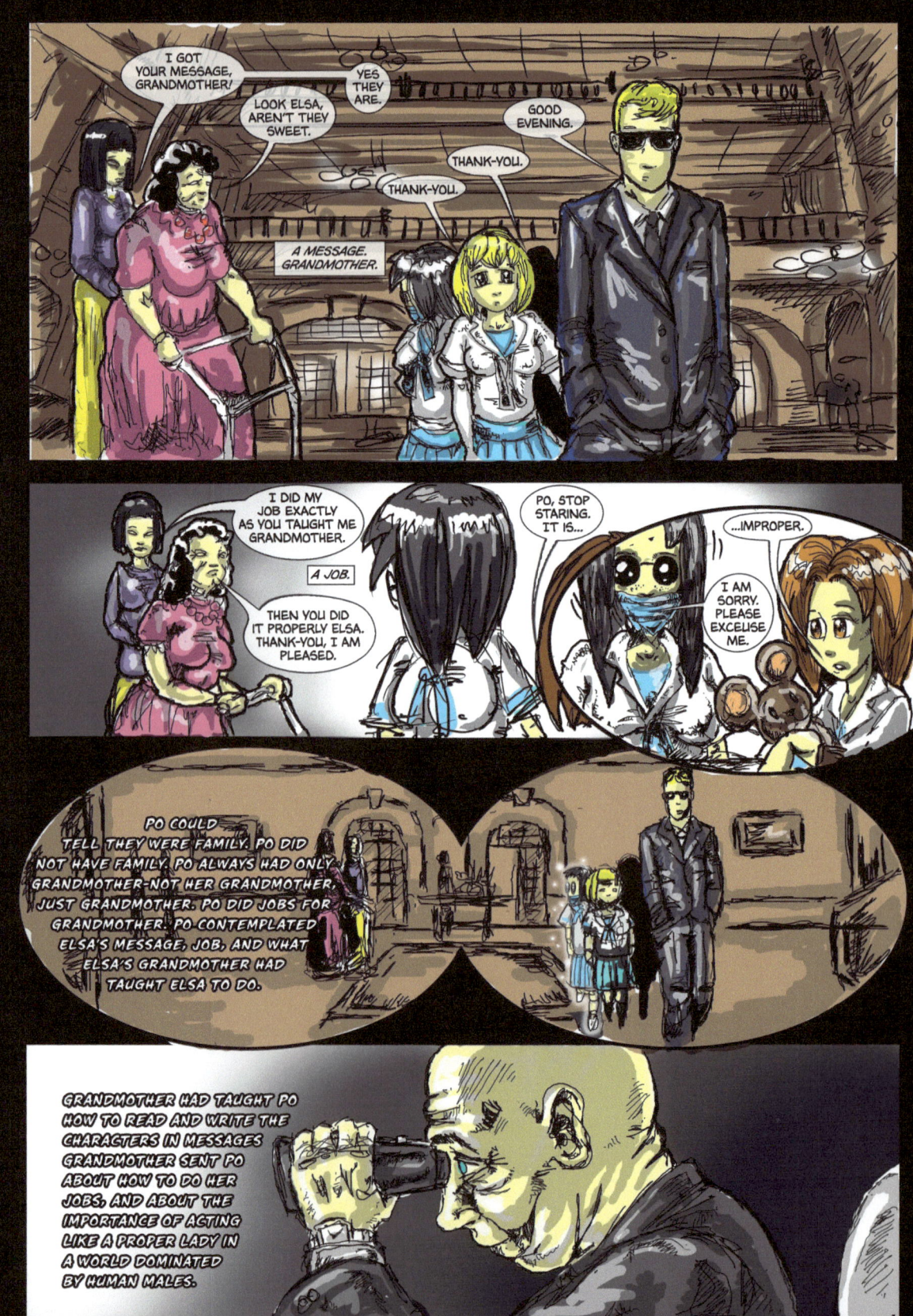

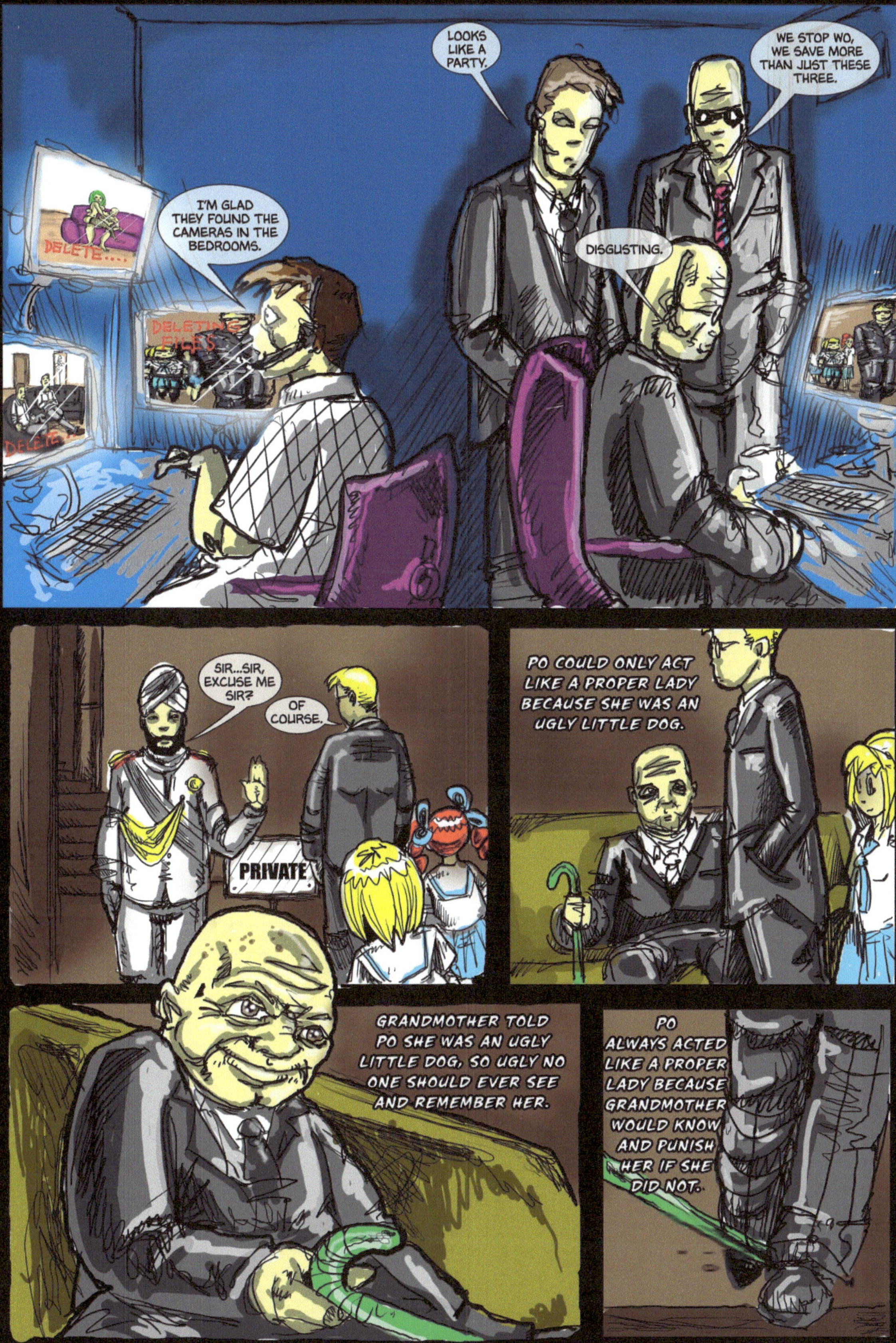
LOOKS LIKE A PARTY.
WE STOP WO, WE SAVE MORE THAN JUST THESE THREE.
I'M GLAD THEY FOUND THE CAMERAS IN THE BEDROOMS.
DISGUSTING.
DELETE....
DELETING FILES
SIR...SIR, EXCUSE ME SIR?
OF COURSE.
PRIVATE
PO COULD ONLY ACT LIKE A PROPER LADY BECAUSE SHE WAS AN UGLY LITTLE DOG.
GRANDMOTHER TOLD PO SHE WAS AN UGLY LITTLE DOG, SO UGLY NO ONE SHOULD EVER SEE AND REMEMBER HER.
PO ALWAYS ACTED LIKE A PROPER LADY BECAUSE GRANDMOTHER WOULD KNOW AND PUNISH HER IF SHE DID NOT.

SIMI LAN JO/*

"WHAT THE FUCK", IN SINGLISH, COLLOQUIAL SINGAPOREAN ENGLISH.

COMMODORE!

SAW YOUR SIGNAL, OLE BOY... ...INCOGNITO, EH?

≥Snicker/≤

≥Ha ha ha/≤

≥Giggle/≤ EXCUSE ME.

≥Giggle/≤ EXCUSE ME.

≥Ha ha ha/≤

≥Ha ha ha/≤

≥Ha ha ha/≤

22:55

≥Ha ha ha/≤

≥Ha ha ha/≤

≥Ha ha ha/≤

≥Ha ha ha/≤

SOMETIMES GRANDMOTHER CALLED PO AN UGLY LITTLE DOG AND PUNISHED PO, AND PO WOULD NOT KNOW WHY.

≥Ha ha ha/≤

≥Ha ha ha/≤

≥Ha ha ha/≤

22:58

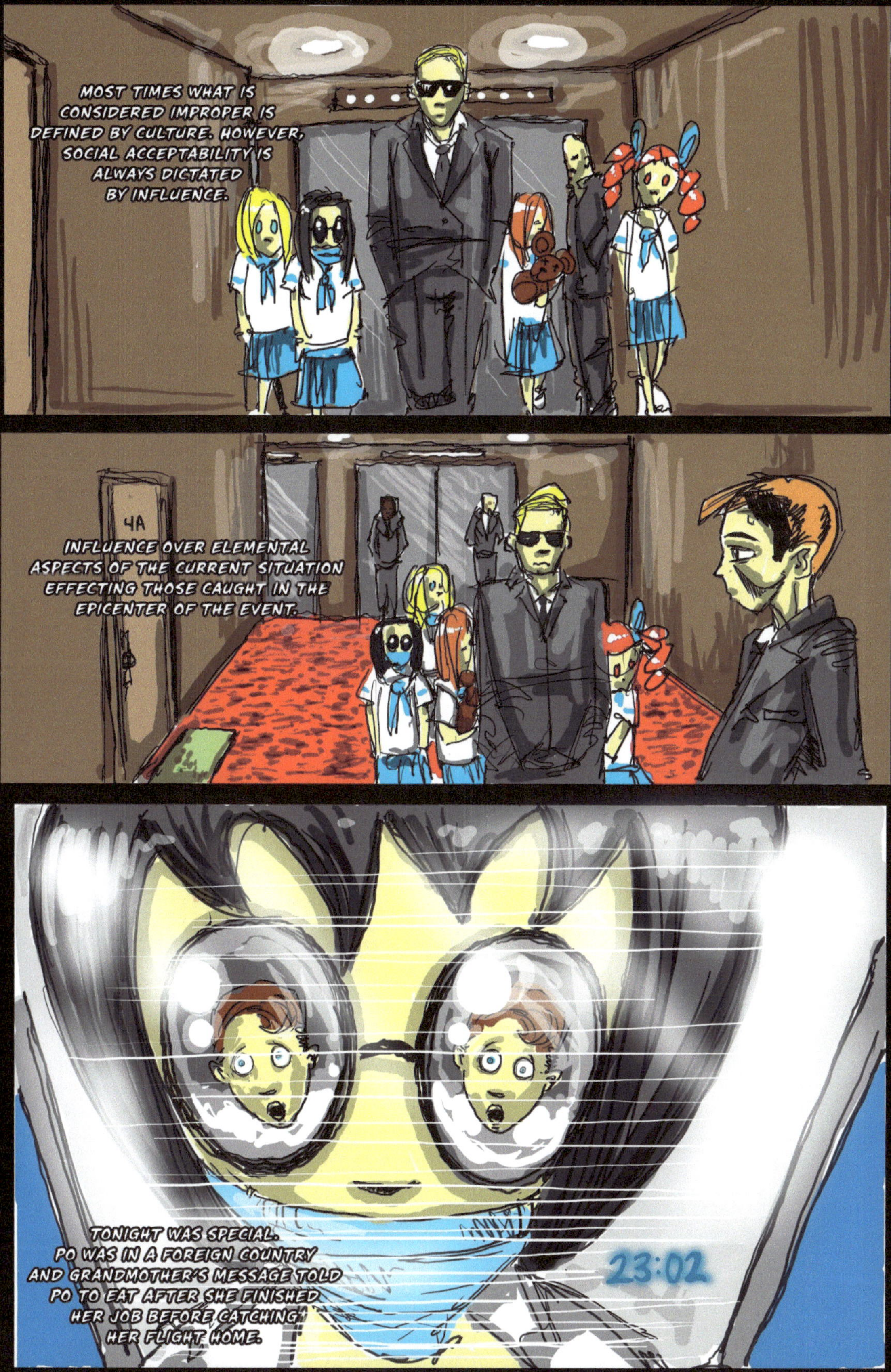

MOST TIMES WHAT IS CONSIDERED IMPROPER IS DEFINED BY CULTURE. HOWEVER, SOCIAL ACCEPTABILITY IS ALWAYS DICTATED BY INFLUENCE.

INFLUENCE OVER ELEMENTAL ASPECTS OF THE CURRENT SITUATION EFFECTING THOSE CAUGHT IN THE EPICENTER OF THE EVENT.

TONIGHT WAS SPECIAL. PO WAS IN A FOREIGN COUNTRY AND GRANDMOTHER'S MESSAGE TOLD PO TO EAT AFTER SHE FINISHED HER JOB BEFORE CATCHING HER FLIGHT HOME.

23:02

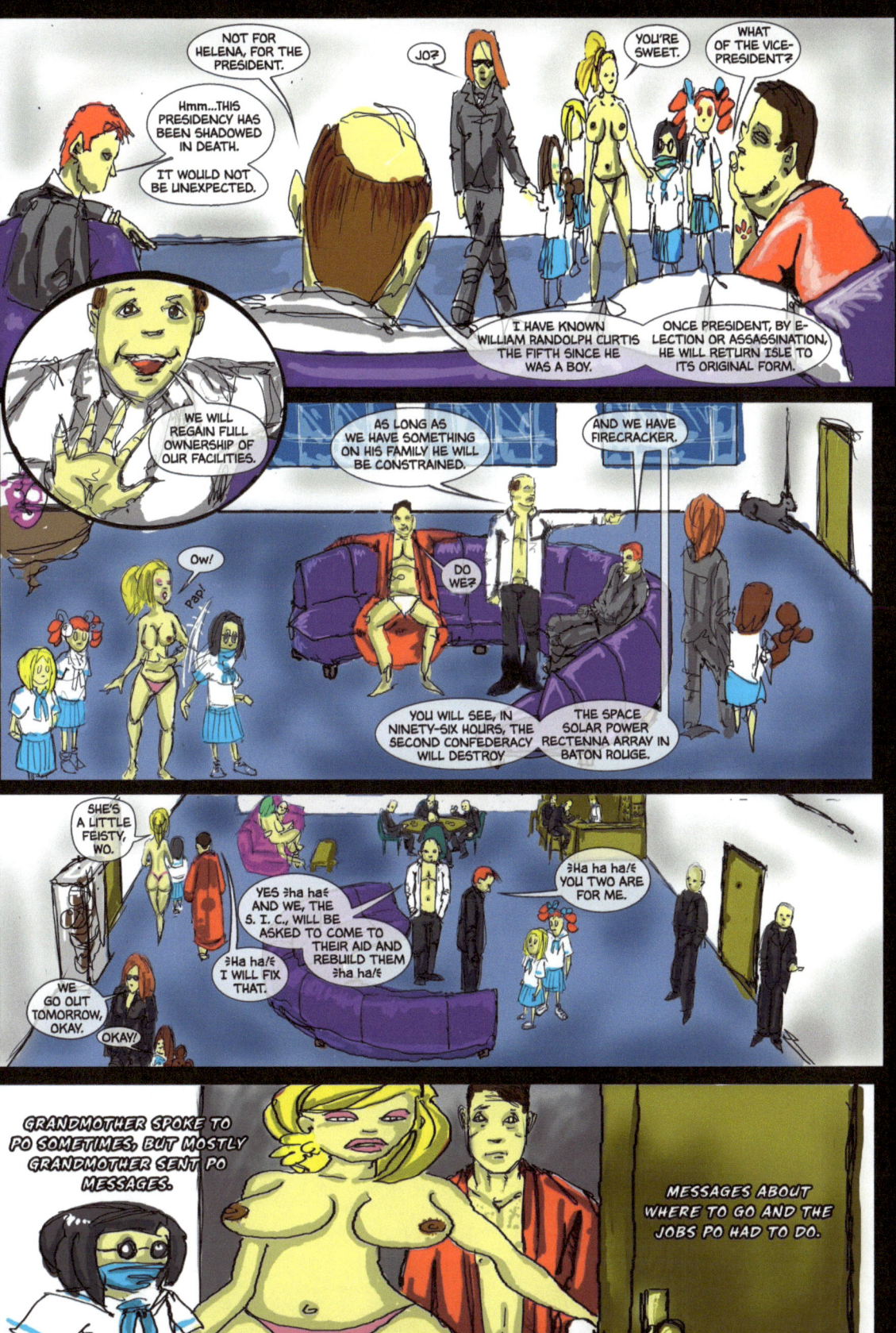

PISTOLS, KNIVES, SWORDS, POISON, BOMBS WERE FUN; PO'S FAVORITE WAS THE RIFLE. PO LIKED LOOKING THROUGH THE RIFLESCOPE. PO NEVER MISSED WITH A RIFLE.

PO HAD BEEN TO SO MANY PLACES AND DONE SO MANY JOBS FOR GRANDMOTHER, WITH SO MANY DIFFERENT TYPES OF WEAPON...

...PO STOPPED COUNTING HER MESSAGES AND JOBS.

THIS JOB WAS DIFFERENT. NO WEAPONS AND GRANDMOTHER'S MESSAGE TOLD PO TO DO THINGS PO HAD NEVER DONE.

PO KNEW SHE WOULD BE PUNISHED IF SHE DID NOT TAKE TIME...

...TO DO THEM ALL.

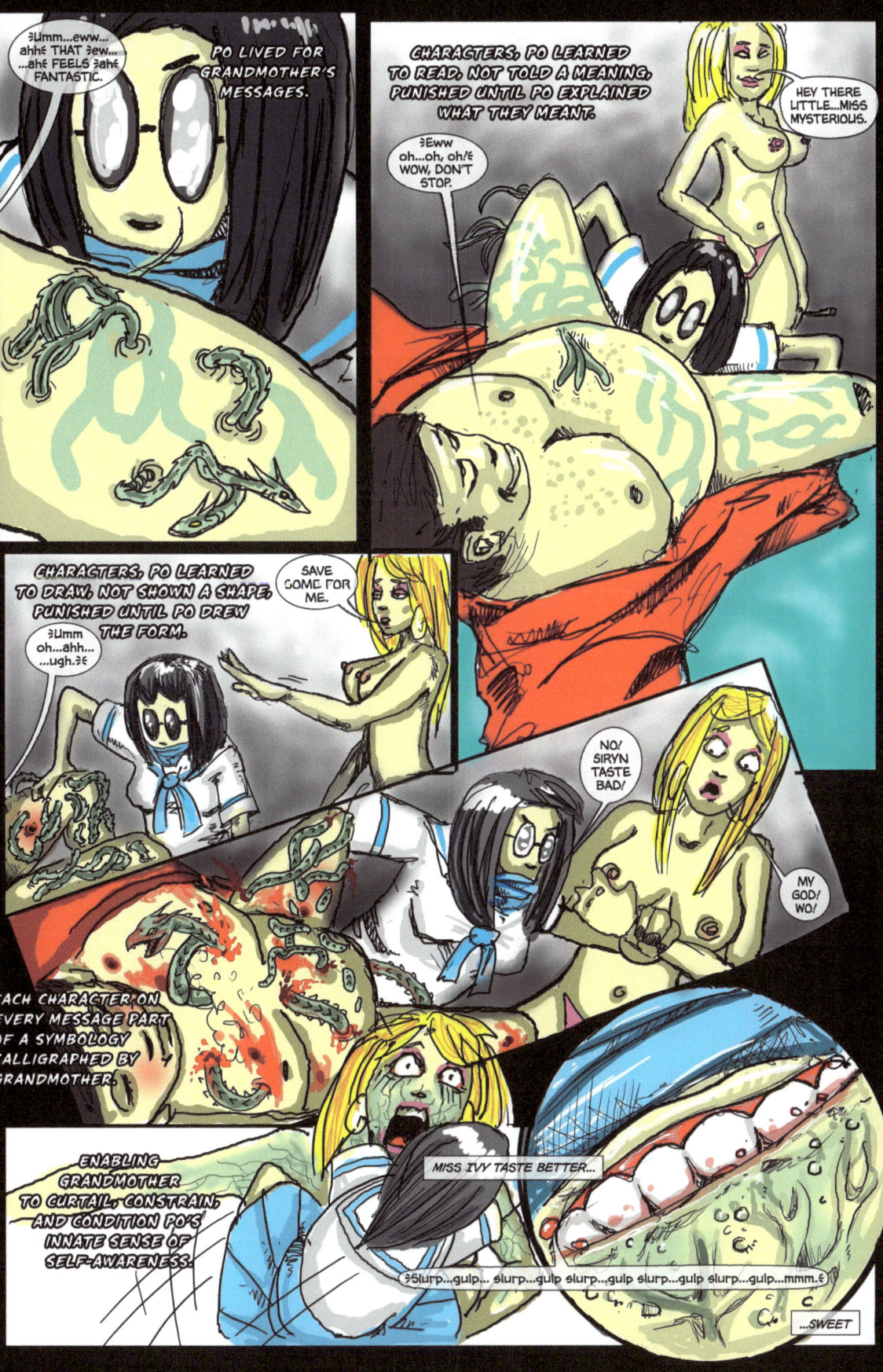

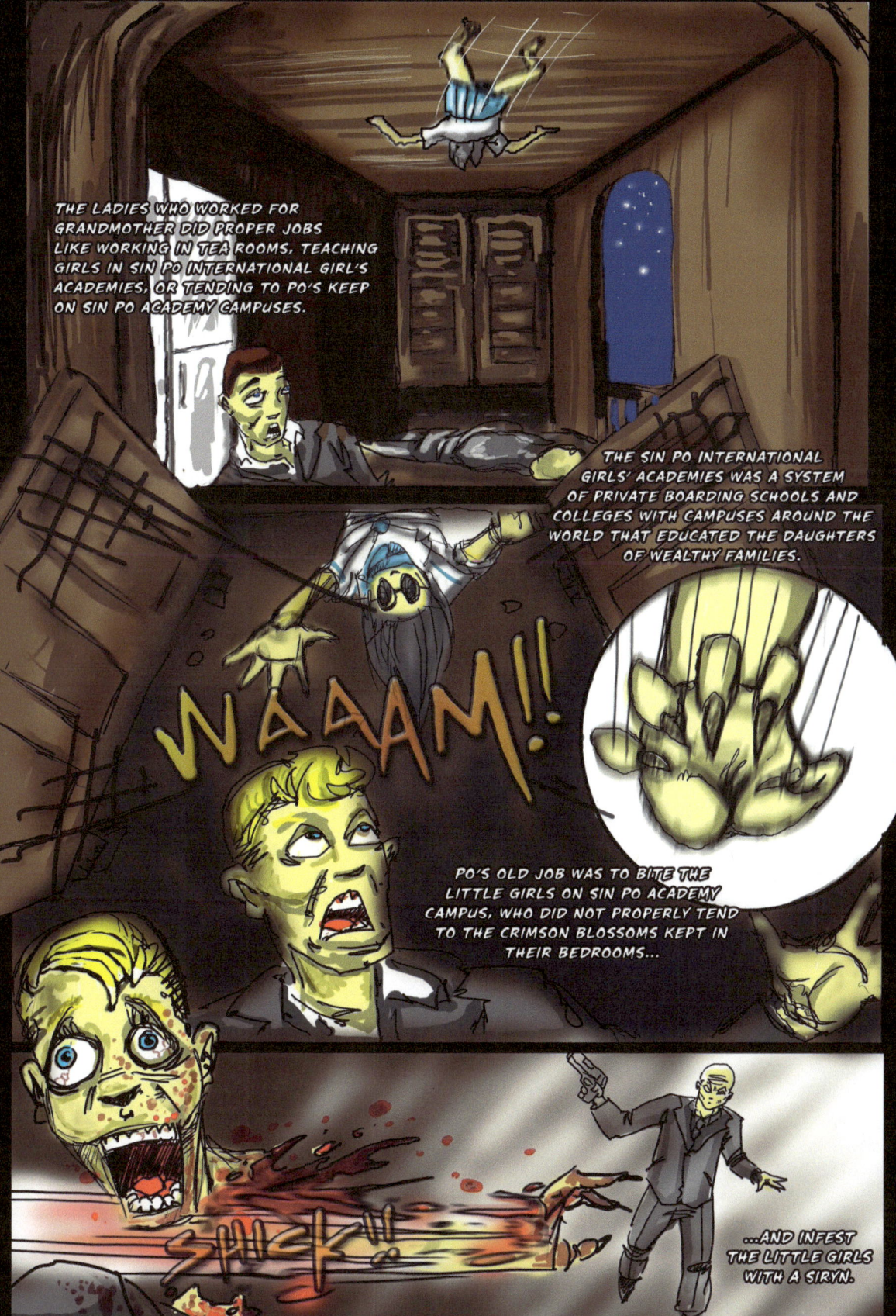

THOUGH THE SIRYN DID NOT DIVIDE, GROW AND CONSUME THEM, AS THE LITTLE GIRLS GREW TO BECOME LADIES, GRANDMOTHER COULD SPEAK TO THE LADIES IN THEIR DREAMS AND THEY WOULD DO PROPER JOBS FOR GRANDMOTHER.

PO DID NOT LIKE HER OLD JOB BECAUSE PO WOULD HAVE TO STAY LEASHED IN A CAGE.

Sqwahiss!

Sqwahiss!

Sqwahiss!

Sqwahiss!

AT NIGHT, ONE OF GRANDMOTHER'S LADIES WOULD LET PO OFF HER LEASH AND OUT OF HER CAGE SO PO COULD DO HER JOB.

Schooluch!

♪Oh ho ho oh.♪

PO LOOKED FORWARD TO BITING THE LITTLE GIRLS BECAUSE NOT ONLY WOULD PO BE LET OFF HER LEASH AND OUT OF HER CAGE; BUT THE LITTLE GIRLS TASTED SWEET AND GIGGLED IN THEIR SLEEP WHEN PO BIT THEM.

FOR YEARS PO DID HER OLD JOB AND LIVED LEASHED IN A CAGE BEING SHIPPED AROUND THE WORLD FROM ONE SIN PO ACADEMY CAMPUS TO ANOTHER BITING LITTLE GIRLS AT NIGHT.

Sqwahiss!

♪Eww.. ahhh...ohhh.. ...umm...ohhh ahhhh.♪

Sqwahiss!

Sqwahiss!

Sqwahiss!

Sqwahiss!

Sqwahiss!

Sqwahiss!

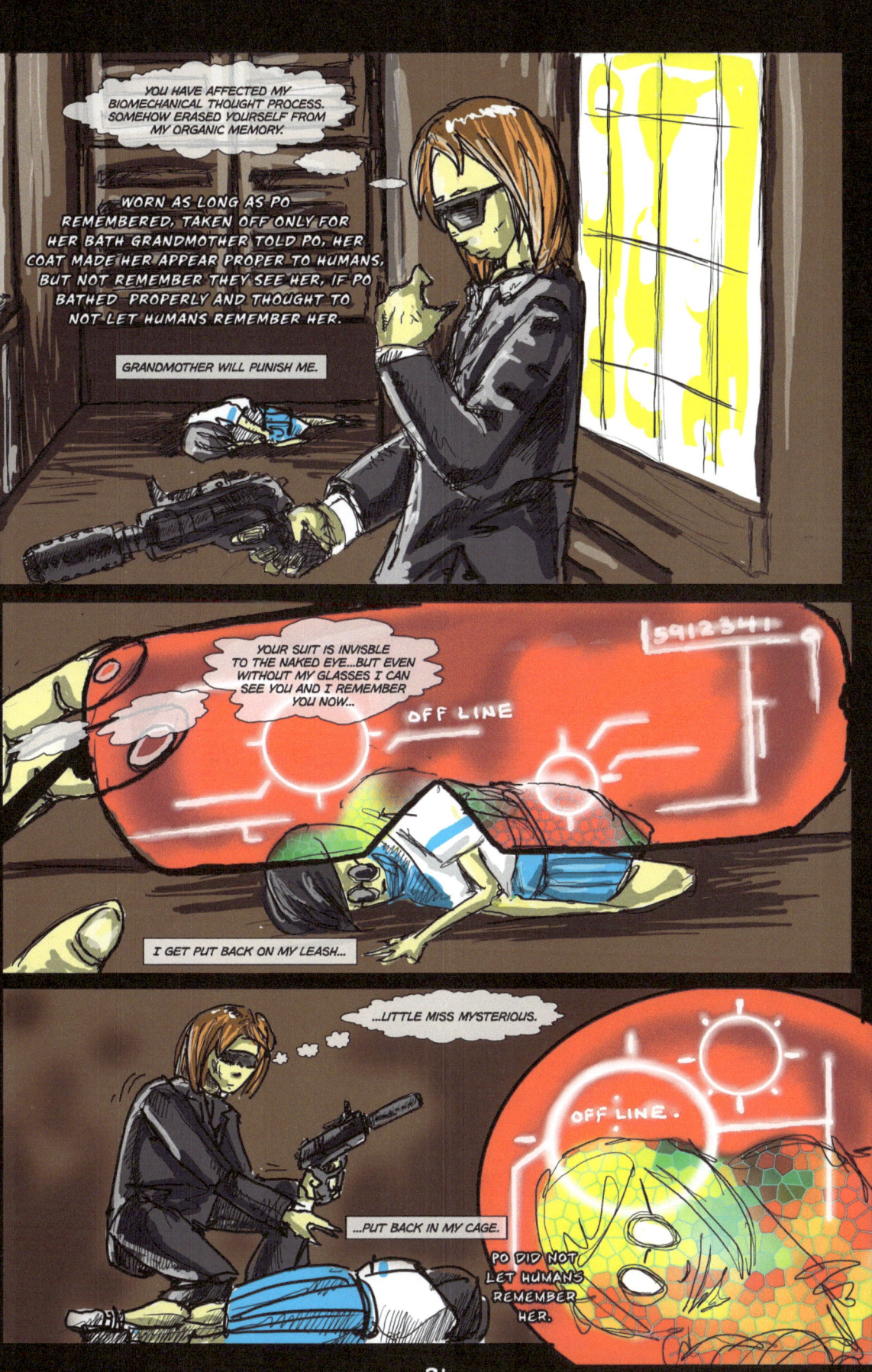

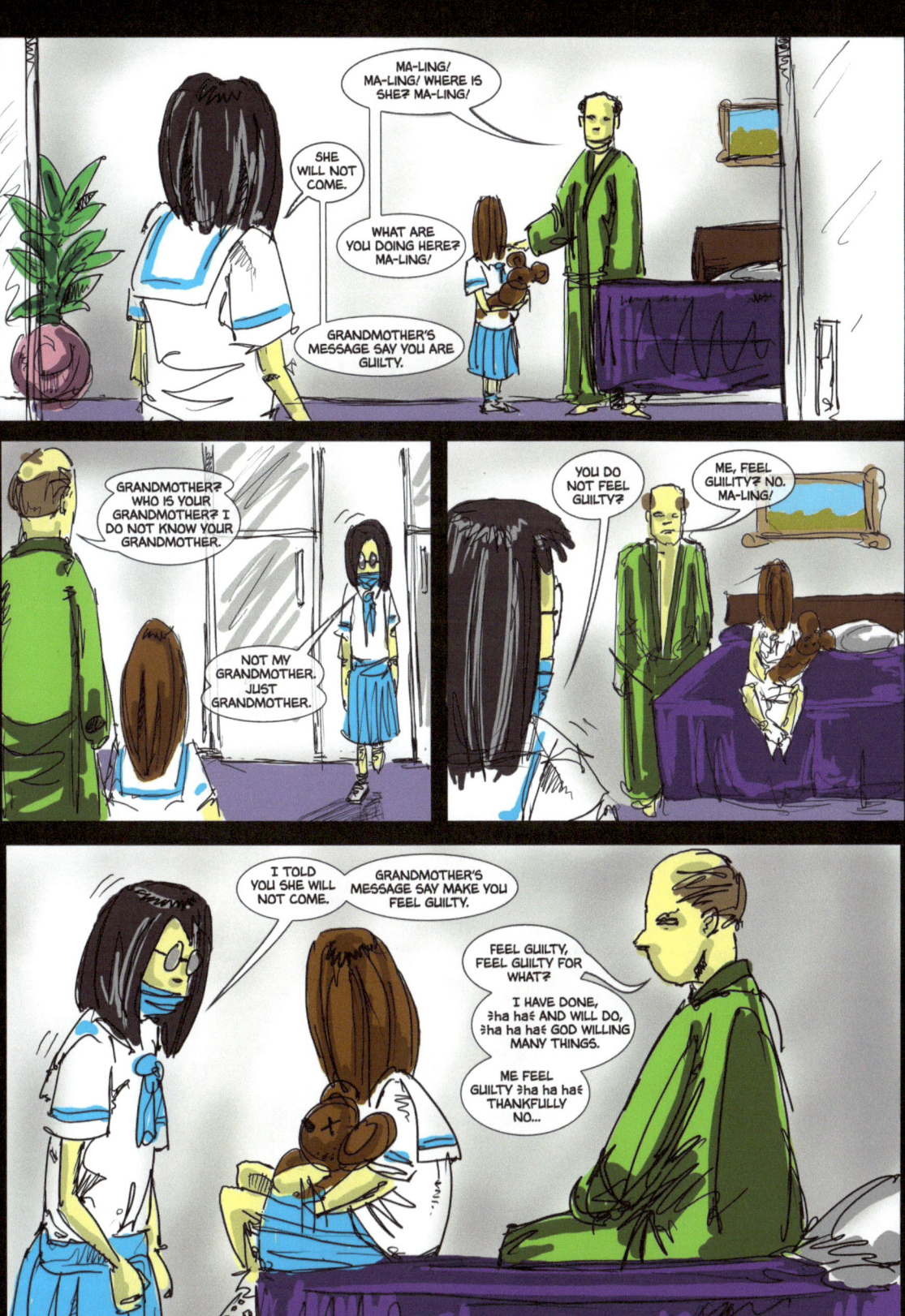

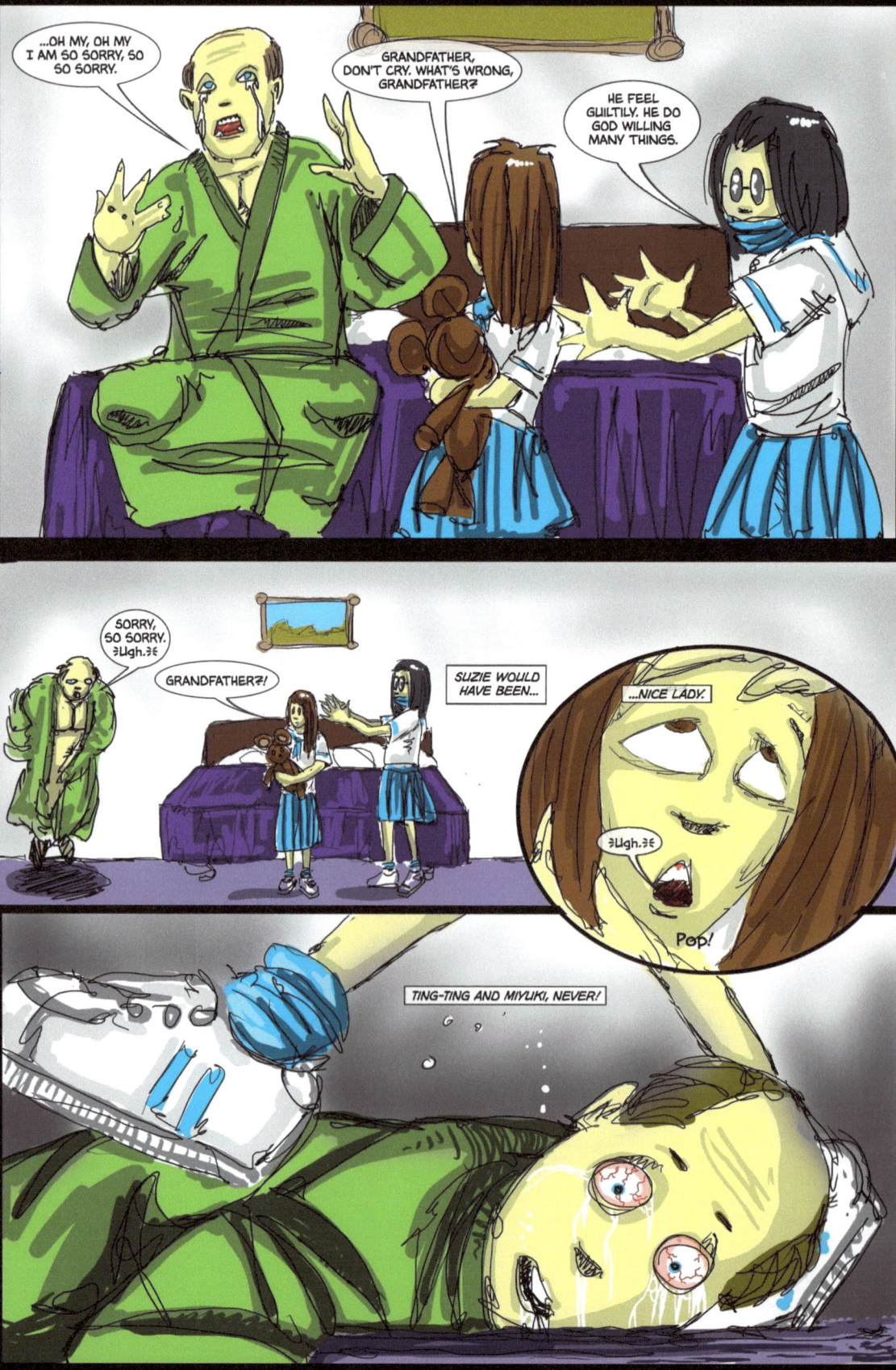

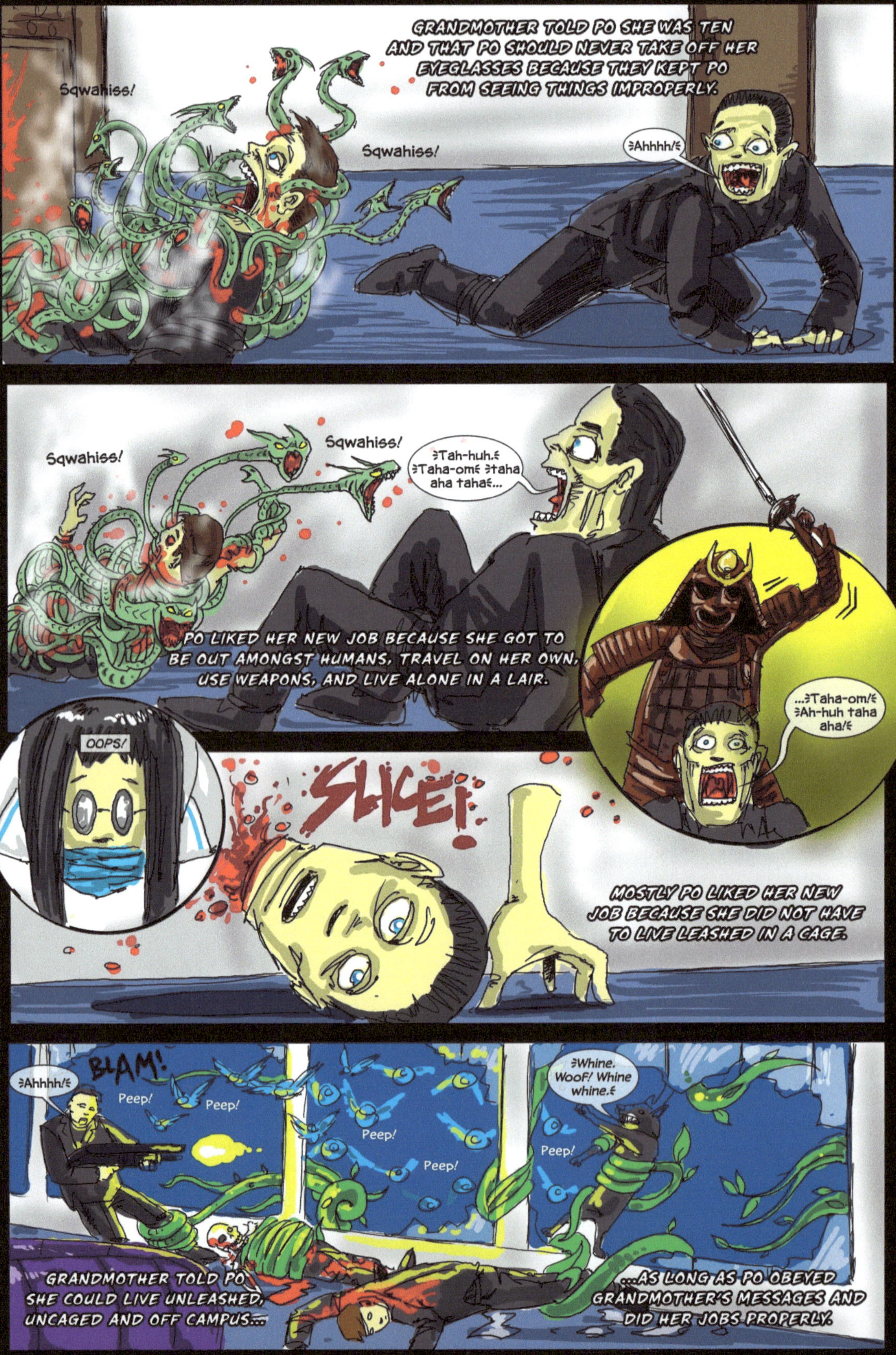

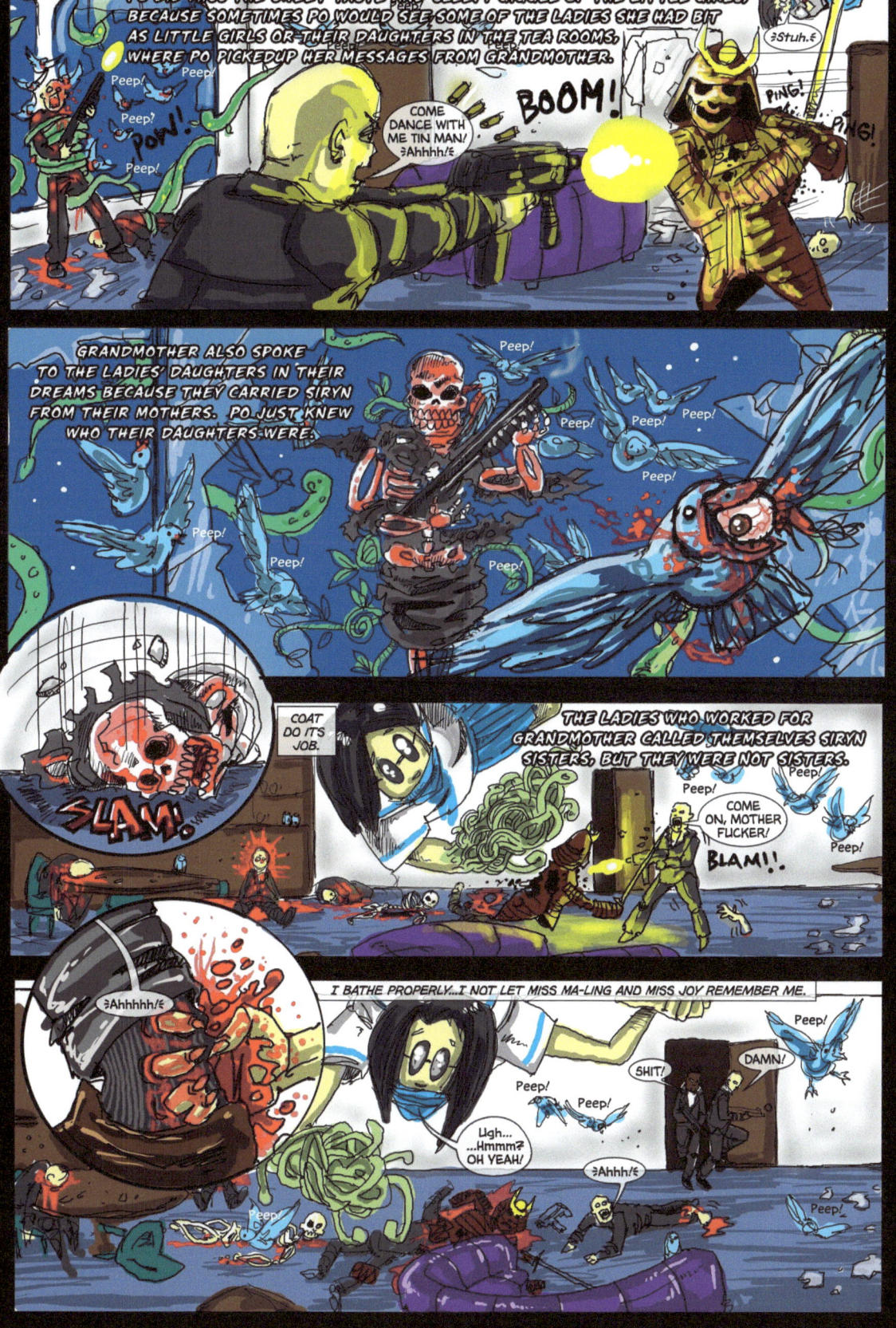

PO KNEW THEY WERE NOT SISTERS BECAUSE
PO HAD NEVER BITTEN TWO DAUGHTERS FROM THE
SAME FAMILY AND SIRYN SISTERS COULD ONLY
PASS A SIRYN ONCE WHILE GIVING BIRTH.

THE SIRYN SISTERS HAD NO SONS AND NO ONE ELSE KNEW ABOUT GRANDMOTHER
OR THE SIRYN SISTERS EXCEPT FOR GRANDMOTHER'S SIRYN BONDED HUMAN MALES.

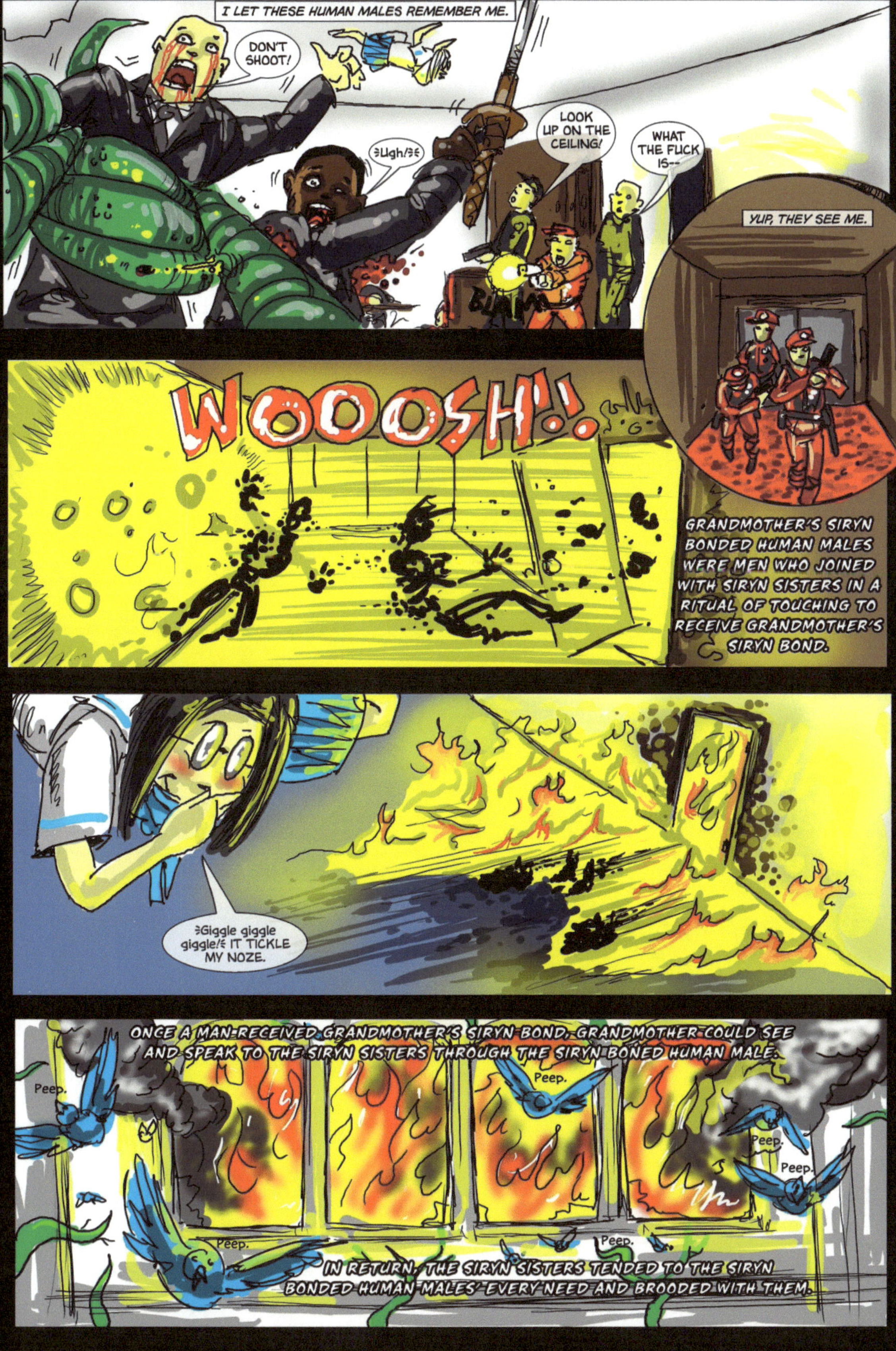

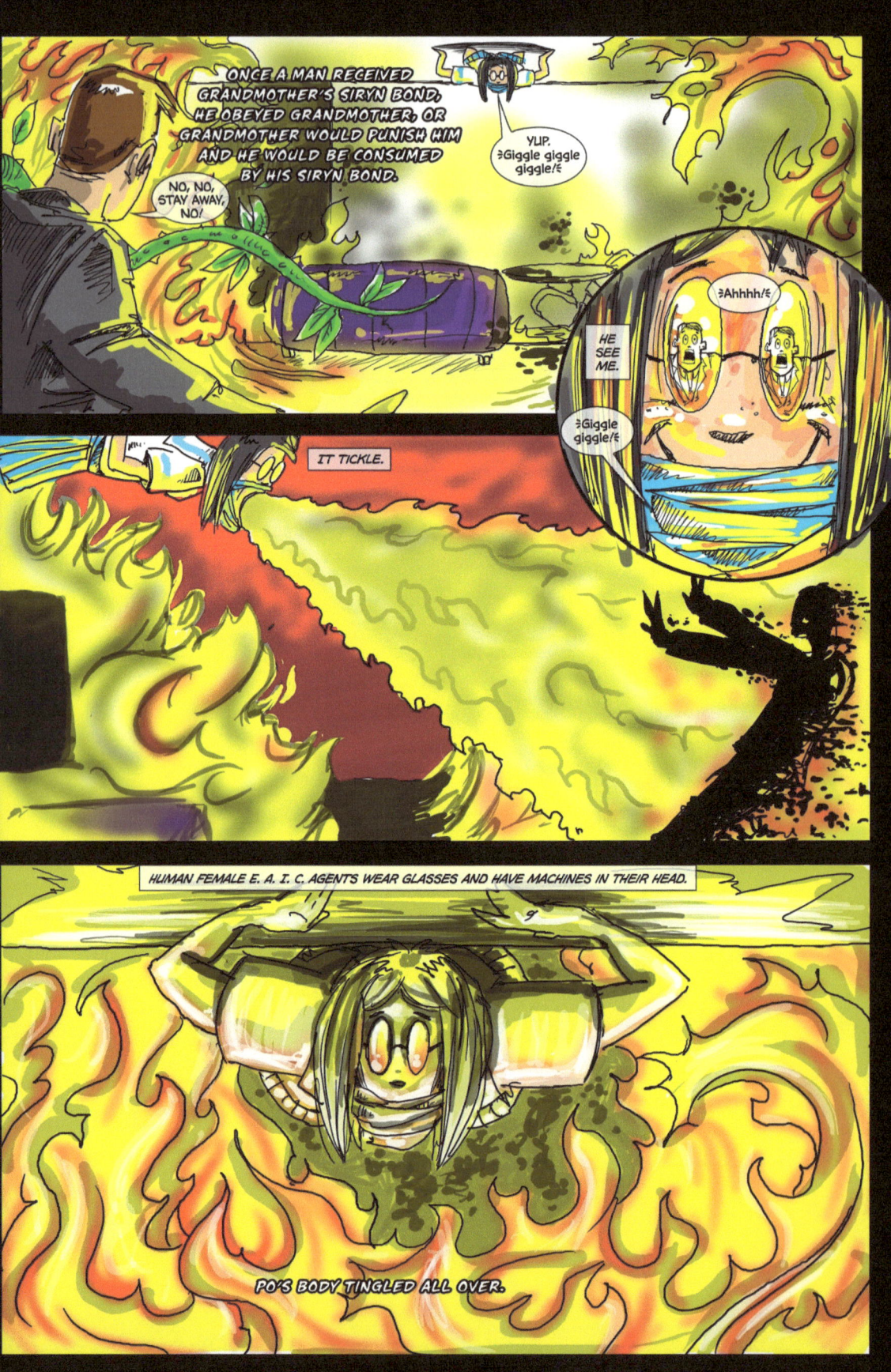

PO HAD NEVER DONE A JOB WITHOUT A WEAPON BEFORE.
CYBERNETIC IMPLANTS.
PO LIKED IT MORE THAN THE RIFLE.
THAT IS WHY MISS MA-LING AND MISS JOY REMEMBER THEY SEE ME.
PO HAD NEVER BEEN EXCITED BEFORE.
BUT GRANDMOTHER WILL PUNISH ME.
ALL PO NEEDED TO DO BEFORE HER RIDE ARRIVED...
23:22
...WAS EAT.

PHILADELPHIA. QUITE THE YOUNG LADY TO BE TRAVELING SO FAR ALL ALONE.
PANG HAVE SIRYN BOND...
I AM ANNA, ANYTHING YOU NEED JUST ASK.
YES, THANK-YOU.
...WHERE PANG SIRYN SISTERS?
THANK-YOU, MISS ANNA, I WILL NOT.
FOR THE FIRST TIME PO WAS INNATELY SELF-AWARE. CONJECTURING FREE WILL ON HER OWN ACCORD; HER THOUGHTS DISTURBED HER.

FOR THE FIRST TIME PO'S MIND WAS CONFUSED.
PALANQUIN
FOR THE FIRST TIME PO FELT ALONE IN DARKNESS.
NOBODY EVER REMEMBER...
...ME?

PO LYN LEE
OPHELIA HOUSE
NEXT ISSUE

"THE SECOND CONFEDERACY"

AFTER SUCCESSFULLY COMPLETING THE S. I. C.
JOB, PO RETURNS TO PHILADELPHIA
ANTICIPATING PUNISHMENT FROM
GRANDMOTHER. IN MEMORIAL TO THE S. I. C.,
FIRECRACKER AND THE SECOND
CONFEDERACY MOVE TO EXECUTE THEIR PLAN
TO DESTROY THE SPACE SOLAR POWER
RECTENNA ARRAY IN BATON ROUGE. AS
PANG'S CLOCK TICKS DOWN, PO RECEIVES
ANOTHER MESSAGE.

CARLTON L. SAMPSON

POET, GRAPHIC NOVELL AUTHOR
CARLTON@POLYNLEE.COM
OTHER WORK AVAILABLE AT:
WWW.PHASCISTCLOWNS.COM

ANDREW L. WILLIS

AKA, THIOBIS THE ARTIST
FINE ART, SCULPTURE, ANIMATION,
MUSIC, AND WRITTEN.
ANDREW@POLYNLEE.COM
OTHER WORK AVAILABLE AT:
WWW.WAOOBAKEARTWORK.COM

PHILADELPHIA
CENTER CITY

AFTER SUCCESSFULLY COMPLETING THE S. I. C. JOB, PO RETURNS TO
PHILADELPHIA ANTICIPATING PUNISHMENT FROM GRANDMOTHER. IN
MEMORIAL TO THE S. I. C., FIRECRACKER AND THE SECOND CONFEDERACY
MOVE TO EXECUTE THEIR PLAN TO DESTROY THE SPACE SOLAR POWER
RECTENNA ARRAY IN BATON ROUGE. AS PANG'S CLOCK TICKS DOWN,
PO RECEIVES ANOTHER MESSAGE.

NEXT ISSUE

WWW.POLYNLEE.COM

www.ingramcontent.com/pod-product-compliance
Lightning Source LLC
Chambersburg PA
CBHW041001170626
46815CB00002B/97